KUNA & KUNI TAKE FLIGHT

STORIES FROM PIPLIVAN ~ 1

STORY
GOURI DASH

ILLUSTRATIONS
RATNA MORINIAUX REGE

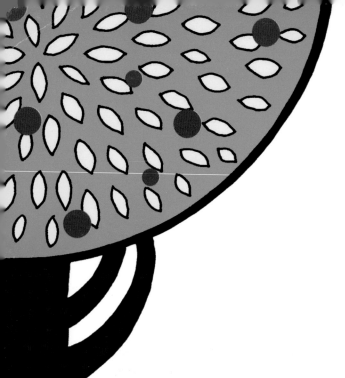

ISBN 978-93-80154-97-8
© Text Gouri Dash, 2010
© Illustrations Ratna Moriniaux Rege, 2010

Design & Layouts Kinny Kaul, Mind's Eye, Mumbai
Printing Dhote Offset, Mumbai

Published in India 2010, by
HAPPY SQUIRREL
An imprint of
LEADSTART PUBLISHING PVT LTD
Trade Centre, Level 1
Bandra Kurla Complex
Bandra (E), Mumbai 400 051, INDIA
T + 91 22 40700804
F +91 22 40700800
E info@leadstartcorp.com
W www.leadstartcorp.com

Sales Office
Unit 122, building B/2
Wadala (E), Mumbai 400 037, INDIA
T +91 22 24046887

US Office
Axis Corp
7845 E Oakbrook Circle
Madison, WI 53717, USA

This book is dedicated to the loving memory
of my eldest daughter, the Late Mrs Bharati Rath

About the Storyteller

Gouri Dash is 85 years young, lives in India and spends her time between Mumbai, Pune and Bhubaneshwar. She has been a published author in regional languages for over three decades and her stories have entertained and fascinated young readers over generations. Her work has been included in the curricular of several State Boards in India.

Additionally, her translations from Bengali to Oriya, of the works of the renowned Bengali author, Asha Purna Devi, have won her many accolades. She has also translated eighteen books of her guru, Sri Sri Sitaramdas Omkarnath Maharaj, from Bengali to Oriya

When she is not writing, Gouri enjoys reading, cooking good food and feeding everyone around her and narrating ageless stories to her grandchildren and great grandchildren.

This story is her first attempt at writing for children in English.

About the Illustrator

For **Ratna Rege-Moriniaux**, painting has always been a passion. After a degree in Fine Arts (Applied Arts) from the J. J. School of Arts, Mumbai, she worked for a long period as an Art Director in Ambience Advertising in Mumbai. Ratna moved to France after her marriage and now heads an art workshop in a centre for mentally handicapped people. In her spare time she pursues her passion for art. She has also recently illustrated the children's book, One Night In The Sunderbans and another in French.

CAST OF CHARACTERS

The Parrot Family
Tuna Father-Parrot
Tuni Mother-Parrot
Kuna & Kuni Twin-Parrots
Guna Grandfather-Parrot
Guni Grandmother-Parrot

Golu, the Priest Dog

Veru, the Tiger Uncle

Bador, the Monkey Uncle

Buru, the Bear

Khari, the Rabbit Aunty

Chatpat, the Squirrel

Teji, the devoted Crow

Shankhi, the wicked Cat

Kuturi, the witty Mouse

Dundul, the singing Frog

Champa, the shy Lizard

Pokari, the smelly boatman Prawn

Manu, the blacksmith Mangoose

Bula, the faithful Dog

Raja, the helpful Kingfisher
&
Gopi, the cunning Cowherd

$\mathcal{L}$ong, long ago, in the land people call Inde, there grew a vast forest which was known as Piplivan. It was a wild and wonderful place full of many kinds of plants and trees, all competing with each other to reach up higher and higher to touch the blue sky. The forest was so dense that sunlight could hardly touch the ground. It was always cool in Piplivan, even on a hot summer day. No people lived there. But it was the home of many animals and birds, all of whom lived together in harmony and happiness. They were the Piplis.

THE NAMING CEREMONY

Among those who belonged to the forest of Piplivan, was a friendly and much-loved parrot-couple called Tuna and Tuni. They had just been blessed with twins – a son and a daughter. There was great excitement as the good news travelled like wildfire and reached all the inhabitants of the forest.

The Head Priest of Piplivan was Golu the Dog. He had become obese because he just loved lying around without doing any work the whole day long. As usual he was fast asleep and had to be woken up and summoned to make a horoscope for the new baby Parrots and to decide on a good day to have the naming ceremony.

Golu finally got up with great reluctance, opened his big, black umbrella and sat under it and put on his glasses.

Then he took out the almanac to cast the horoscopes of the babies, which would tell everyone what they would become when they grew up and left the nest. Golu then decided the day for the naming ceremony, quickly recited some verses to bless the newborn children and promised to arrive on time to conduct the ceremony. Then he took off his glasses, closed his book and umbrella, curled up and went back to sleep.

The eagerly awaited day of the naming ceremony finally dawned and what a gathering it was! Veru, the usually fierce Tiger Uncle, distributed sweets to everyone. He looked particularly handsome dressed in a brand new suit.

Bador, Monkey Uncle, brought heaps of green guavas to the feast and everyone was much impressed with his new pair of pink goggles.

Buru the Bear, brought a huge honeycomb which had all the children begging him for a lick. Chatpat Squirrel arrived carrying juicy, sweet berries and Rabbit Aunty Khari, came holding bright orange carrots, still smelling of the fresh earth.

At last everyone gathered in a circle. Golu the Priest recited the sacred words and then offered prayers to the God of All Living Things. Then Grandmother-Parrot Guni & Grandfather-Parrot Guna came forward and proudly announced the names of their newborn grandchildren – Kuna and Kuni. Everyone cheered – the noise could be heard throughout the forest! Then it was time for everyone to sit down to eat… and eat… and eat.

THE CAPTURE OF KUNA & KUNI

Kuna and Kuni grew quickly and became naughtier by the day. Mother-

Parrot Tuni, stayed home to keep an eye on them as there were no

babysitters in Piplivan. Father-Parrot Tuna, had the job

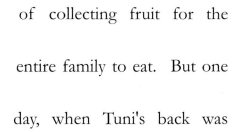

of collecting fruit for the

entire family to eat. But one

day, when Tuni's back was

turned, Kuna and Kuni quietly hopped out

of the nest and tried to spread their wings to fly. When Tuni saw them

tottering on the branch, she scolded them for going outside alone. But she

was secretly pleased that they were such a brave pair of Parrots. That night

she told them they must wait a little longer till their wings became strong.

Then they could fly and be free! They were so excited they could hardly

wait.

One day Father-Parrot Tuna had flown a long way to another forest, to attend a friend's wedding and Tuni was all alone with the children. They were hungry and there was no food left, so she decided to fetch some fruit herself. She strictly instructed the children not to step out till she returned.

Tuni had not left their nest since the twins were born and did not know which trees were bearing fruit. She kept flying from tree to tree in search of good fruit – but all in vain. Back at the nest Kuna and Kuni were getting very hungry and began to shove each other and quarrel loudly.

Gopi the Cowherd had come to the grassy slopes near Piplivan to graze his cattle and saw the two little Parrots chirping loudly with hunger.

He quietly spread a net under the tree and put a ripe guava on top of the net.

Kuna, who was the impatient one, saw the fruit first and at once wanted to

go to eat it. Kuni, who was more cautious, stopped him. But Kuna was too

hungry and too naughty to listen to her. He fluttered down to the ground

and went to eat the guava. At once Gopi threw the net over him and he was

caught in the trap! Seeing her brother in trouble, Kuni could not stay back

and hopped down to rescue her brother. But she too got trapped in the net.

TEJI FINDS A CLUE

When Mother-Parrot Tuni returned to the nest with the fruit she had finally found, Father-ParrotTuna had already returned from the wedding and was looking everywhere for his family, who were nowhere to be found. Seeing Tuni fly in, he felt relieved. But where were Kuna and Kuni? When they realized their children were missing, they started searching frantically.

Tuna sent a message through the Birdcall Post to all the birds in the entire forest to organize a search to find the missing children. Soon every bird in Piplivan had joined the search party.

Tuni's best friend, Teji the Crow, came back to report that she had seen Gopi the Cowherd holding a cage, but she could not see inside it as it was covered with a towel. The birds decided on a plan and sent Teji back. She flew down and pecked at the Cowherd's head with her sharp beak.

Gopi fell down with the cage and Teji was able to spot Kuna and Kuni huddled together inside. She quickly flew back to the forest with the news and then led Tuna and Tuni to the hut where Gopi the Cowherd lived.

By the time they reached the hut, it was already evening and Gopi had taken the cage inside the house for the night. The Parrot parents Tuna and Tuni, along with their friend Teji, had no other option but to wait outside the house on the branch of a tree.

As morning came, Gopi awoke and came out of the hut to hang the cage outside before taking his cattle out to graze. Tuna and Tuni immediately flew down to calm the frightened children.

They brought them fruit and water and told

them to have courage while they planned

the escape.

Just then, around the corner of the hut came

Sankhi, Gopi's pet cat. Seeing the birds in the cage she

jumped up and tried to catch hold of the twins. But try as she could, Sankhi

could not reach them. The Parrot parents saw Sankhi and became most

worried. They knew they had to act fast to save the children. But how?

DUNDUL, KUTURI & CHAMPA
JOIN THE RESCUE

Tuni finally told Tuna to find her old friend Kuturi the Mouse, and ask for

her help to free the children. Tuni knew she lived in the Bamboo grove at

Piplivan but did not have her exact address. So Tuna flew to the Bamboo

grove. But, it was too dark and dense and there was no trace of Kuturi.

Just as he was about to turn back, he heard someone singing, Sa Re Ga Ma

Pa Dha Ni Sa. The music was coming from an old hut with a broken door

standing open. Tuna carefully hopped in to find Dundul the old Frog

singing and playing a Harmonium. Dundul was most annoyed with Tuna

for disturbing him at his singing practice. But when he heard Tuna's story,

Dundul soon calmed down.

Tuna requested him to help locate Kuturi's house. Dundul started laughing

and said she was his neighbour! Kuturi the Mouse lived right next door,

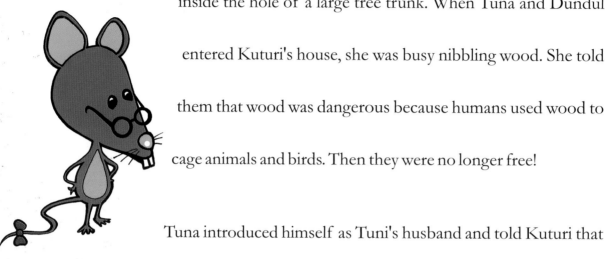

inside the hole of a large tree trunk. When Tuna and Dundul

entered Kuturi's house, she was busy nibbling wood. She told

them that wood was dangerous because humans used wood to

cage animals and birds. Then they were no longer free!

Tuna introduced himself as Tuni's husband and told Kuturi that

her young friend was in need of her help. Kuturi could not stop her tears

rolling down her wrinkled face when she heard the plight of the children.

She immediately took Tuna and Dundul to her friend Champa, the Lizard,

who lived on a tree nearby. Champa covered herself in leaves to hide but

when Kuturi called to her, she slowly came out from under the leaves. She

welcomed them to her house in the fork of the tree and served them sun-

roasted insects, which Dundul immediately gobbled up. Tuna was a pure

vegetarian so he skipped the snack.

After a lot of discussion it was decided that Kuturi would gnaw

through the wooden cage with her sharp teeth and free the

children. But she told Tuna, Dundul and Champa that

she was not sure how much time it would take her

to accomplish this as her teeth had become

blunt due to the amount of wood she had

been nibbling on. Dundul then had a

bright idea! He said that Kuturi could get

her teeth sharpened with

the help of her brother-in-

law, Manu the Mongoose, who

was a blacksmith. Kuturi smiled

at such a clever idea!

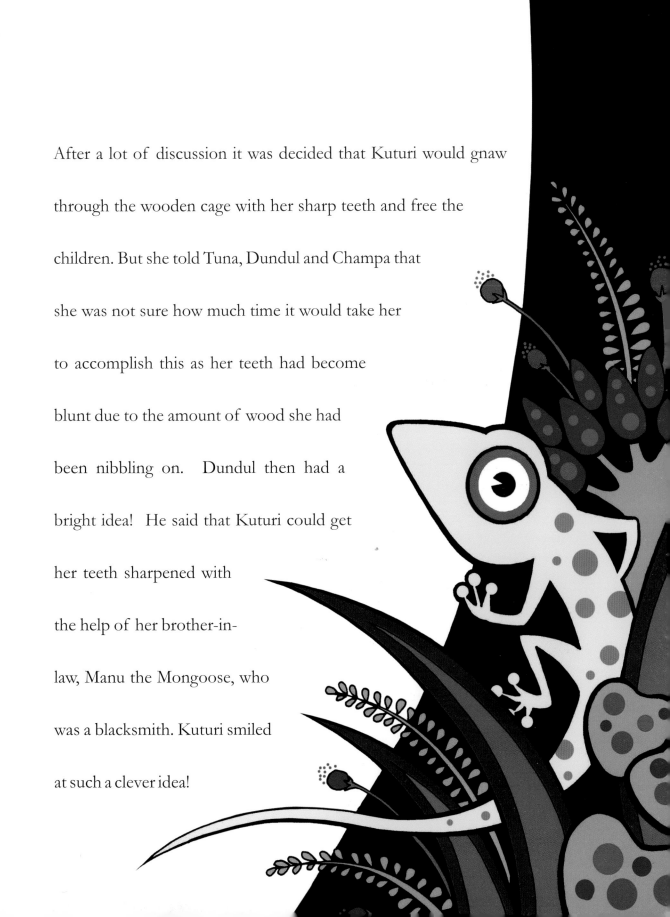

MEETING MANU & POKHARI

Manu lived across a muddy river which they had to cross early the next morning when the water would be calm. To make the crossing they needed the help of Pokhari the old Prawn, the only good boatman in Piplivan. Nobody liked Pokhari because he was irritable and grumpy and stank all the time. No one talked to him so he lived alone near the river. But Tuna had no choice but to beg old Pokhari to help them cross the river.

Tuna did not waste any more time but hurried to Pokhari's boat and asked for his help. Pokhari was not too happy to have Kuturi in his boat because she never said anything good about him. But finally he agreed to help because he loved the Parrot children.

Early next morning, just as dawn was breaking, Tuna, Dundul, Kuturi and Champa boarded Pokhari's boat and crossed the stream to reach Manu's

house. When Manu heard how Gopi the Cowherd

had trapped Kuna and Kuni, he muttered angrily

under his breath and quickly began to sharpen

Kuturi's teeth. He then wished them good-luck and

they started on their mission immediately.

THE ESCAPE

All this time Mother-Parrot Tuni had been keeping watch from a custard apple tree. She hoped Father-Parrot Tuna had found her friend Kuturi. But when evening fell and Tuna did not return with help, Tuni became very worried.

Gopi the Cowherd again took the cage into the hut for the night. But this time Kuna and Kuni felt a lot braver knowing their mother was on the tree outside. The next morning Gopi did not bring the cage outside when he left to go graze his cattle. Kuna and Kuni were left inside the hut.

Just then Tuni heard the fluttering of wings and saw Tuna returning and with him came Kuturi, Dundul and Champa too. She rushed to meet her old friend Kuturi and begged her to start cutting through the cage without losing another moment! But Dundul stopped her. He reminded everyone

that they had to first think of a clever plan to free the children since Sankhi the Cat would be prowling around and would pose a danger to Kuturi's life while she was gnawing on the wooden cage.

Champa the Lizard suggested they should get hold of Bula, Gopi's old dog who was Sankhi the Cat's sworn enemy as he had been chased out of Gopi's hut once Sankhi entered. Tuna met Bula and convinced him to join in the rescue. Bula was ready to help but the problem was how to get Sankhi away from the hut? Bula suddenly had an idea! He suggested they get some fish which Sankhi could not resist and place it behind the hut. Then one of them could tell Sankhi about it. She would certainly go off to find such a tasty meal. The plan was perfect!

Tuna flew quickly to his childhood friend, Raja the Kingfisher, and told him the whole story. Could he get the fish they needed? Raja was happy to help and got Tuna some fish from the pond, and wrapped it in lotus leaves. Waving a quick goodbye, Tuna dashed back to the others waiting near the hut. They carefully opened the lotus leaves and laid the fish in the backyard behind the hut. Then they all quickly hid and waited.

Sankhi was sunbathing at the front of the hut when Dundul the Frog hopped up to her and wished her good morning. He told her she had beautiful brown eyes and was probably the prettiest cat he had ever seen. Sankhi smiled and arched her back. Dundul then sat down beside her in the sun and told her how he had seen a bird dropping some fish from its beak into the backyard when he was coming over. Did Sankhi like fish? Sankhi did not wait. She rushed round to the backyard and found the fish.

At once Kuturi and Champa entered the hut and closed the door. Behind the hut Bula was waiting for his revenge. Just as Sankhi took her first mouthful of fish and was enjoying the taste, Bula pounced on her. Sankhi dropped the fish and ran for her life! Bula laughed happily and then sat guarding the hut, making sure no one entered till the children were free.

Kuturi quickly climbed up to the cage. Kuna and Kuni stared at her with scared eyes. Kuturi whispered to them that she was their mother's friend and that they must stay calm and not make any noise. Then she set to work, quickly gnawing through the cage. The trap door swung open! Kuturi told the little Parrots to be brave and fly by themselves towards the door. Their parents were waiting outside. Looking at each other, Kuna and Kuni flew out into the sunshine. They were free – they could fly!

Tears dropped from Mother-Parrot Tuni's eyes when she saw her children fly out.

Tuna and Tuni thanked each of their friends who had done so much to help rescue their children. They promised everyone a feast in celebration! As the others smiled and watched, the Parrot family flew home together — back to Piplivan where they belonged.

WORDS & MEANINGS

almanac......a book giving good days to hold various events

blacksmith...a person who works with metal

cautious.......careful

dense...........crowded and close together

fierce...........savage, hostile

fluttering.......beating of wings

frantically.....madly

gnaw...........chew, bite

goggles.........spectacles with thick rims

graze...........to feed on grass

grove...........a group of trees

harmonium...a musical instrument with keys and a bellow

harmony......in pleasing relationship with each other

horoscope.....information about someone's future

WORDS & MEANINGS

impressed…..to admire

inhabitants…those who live there

instructed…..told to do something

obese………..very fat

plight………..in trouble

relieved……...to stop worrying

reluctance…. not willing to do

sacred………..respected and belonging to God

shove………...to push roughly

strictly………not to be disobeyed

summoned…called to go somewhere

trapped……...made a prisoner

vast…………..very large

wildfire……...a bush or forest fire which burns very quickly